Anonymous

Novenas, hymns and litanies

in honour of St. Francis of Assisi and St. Clare

Anonymous

Novenas, hymns and litanies
in honour of St. Francis of Assisi and St. Clare

ISBN/EAN: 9783742845412

Manufactured in Europe, USA, Canada, Australia, Japa

Cover: Foto ©Andreas Hilbeck / pixelio.de

Manufactured and distributed by brebook publishing software
(www.brebook.com)

Anonymous

Novenas, hymns and litanies

NOVENAS, HYMNS, AND LITANIES,

IN HONOUR OF

ST. FRANCIS OF ASSISI AND ST. CLARE.

BY A

RELIGIOUS OF THE ORDER OF POOR CLARES.

AUTHOR OF

"ST. FRANCIS AND THE FRANCISCANS," "FLOWERS OF MARY," "HYMNS FOR CHILDREN," ETC. ETC.

INTRODUCTION.

As the object of this little work is merely devotional, it does not seem necessary to say anything of the life of a saint so well known as the seraphic Francis; born at Assisi in the year 1182, he had scarcely attained the age of manhood ere he resolved that God and God alone should be his portion. His father's threats, and his mother's tears, were alike unavailing to deter him from his holy purpose. The wealth and position in society which many might have envied, were cast aside as utterly worthless to one bent on celestial gain, and desiring only the honour which comes from God. The inestimable grace of religious vocation had been given to one worthy of it. There was no hesitation, no reluctance, once the call was heard; none of those excuses of duty to be fulfilled in the world too often the last unreservedly to God, and glad of a plausible and apparently good excuse to escape the pain of self-sacrifice.

But though our saint was called himself to a religious life and was the means of leading many to embrace it, and even to brave the tears and opposition of parents, then, as now, too often unwilling to give their children to God; though he encouraged those who were thus called to offer themselves generously and unreservedly to their crucified Lord; still he knew that there were many whose hearts were burning with high and holy aspirations, who longed for some means of devoting themselves to God, even while their very duty to Him required that they should remain in the world.

A merchant of Lucca named Luchesio with his wife Bona Donna were the first to enter the Third order of St. Francis, the first to enrol themselves in that glorious band which has numbered in its ranks priests, and nobles, peasants, and peers, old and young, rich and poor, many of whom are even now canonized by the Church as examples of super-eminent sanctity.

After a time some of these Tertians formed themselves into religious communities which still exist and prosper; but the great object of Francis in founding his Third Order was, we may suppose, rather to assist those who wished to live holy lives in this world; to cover with the shadow of his mantle, to bless with his hands marked with the stigmata of the Lord Jesus those who might have seemed beyond the reach of such favours. To draw all to God, to whom he was himself so intimately united, was the one great object of his life. Happy they who are willing to avail themselves of the opportunity thus afforded them. No one need be excluded save those who wish to exclude themselves. Rank and wealth need prove no hindrance, since the object of Francis is not that such should renounce their wealth or forsake their position in society, but only that they should have a more abundant means of sanctifying both, and thus furthering their own salvation and promoting the glory of God. Incessant occupations, whether in a secular or ecclesiastical calling will prove no embarrassment to the is himself so ardent a lover of poverty. Why then should any be hindered from embracing the privileges and favours so freely offered to them? Surely it must be no little grace to be under the protection of such a saint; to be associated to so many holy and fervent religious, to share in their tears and labours, in their prayers and love. Let us hasten then to enrol ourselves under the banner of Francis. He asks but little from us and he will give a great deal. As his children we can then offer his merits in a more especial manner to our Lord, and hope for his paternal care in our many necessities. Surely those hands, which it is believed were the first to have been marked with the wounds of Jesus crucified, will not be lifted in vain when he intercedes for his children. Surely that sanctity which obtained from God even while on earth the great grant of the Indulgence of the Portiuncula, and the promise that he should release many of his children from purgatory, will plead now even more effectually for those under his special patronage.

As this little work is merely devotional we have not thought it necessary to give the rule of the Third Order, or the indulgences granted to it, which may be seen elsewhere.

There is also the arch-confraternity of the Cord, which is often confounded with the Third Order, from which however it is entirely distinct. There are no obligations attending enrolment in this confraternity except the usual ones of confession and communion, and investment in the Cord (which must be constantly worn) by a priest duly authorized. The great Franciscan Pope Sixtus V. was the originator and promoter of this devotion, to which very great indulgences are attached.

In conclusion, we offer these little devotions both to religious and seculars. Many are flocking under this shadow of Francis as Tertiaries, or in the confraternity of the Cord. God grant that many more may avail themselves of these privileges ; may become children of the Seraphic Father. His heart, so joyous, so full of love, will receive each with a special tenderness, will treasure each with a special love proportioned to their needs. The prayers for each day of the Novenas at the end of the little consideration, could surely be said by all at their morning and evening the subject of meditation or spiritual reading, for which most devout seculars find some spare time during the day. Nor let it be thought that they are intended exclusively for religious; surely charity, humility and obedience are not less necessary in their measure in the world than in the cloister.

Convent of Poor Clares, Kenmare.
Feast of the Stigmata of S. Francis, 1863.

NOVENA* IN HONOUR
OF
ST. FRANCIS OF ASSISI.

FIRST DAY.

Consideration on the humility of St. Francis of Assisi.

The more St. Francis was esteemed by men, the more he humbled himself. He considered himself the greatest sinner in the world; and his idea of the sanctity of the priesthood was so great that he believed himself utterly unworthy of it, and therefore he would never consent to receive holy

* This Novena (and that which follows it to St. Clare) is translated from those which are used at Ara Cœli, the great church of the Franciscan Fathers at Rome. This Novena to St. Francis may begin on the 25th of September, if said for his feast on the 4th of October, or on the 8th of September if used preparatory to the Feast of the Stigmata.

orders. To deceive those who thought well of him, he made his faults known to all, or ordered one of his companions to overwhelm him with reproaches and insults. He listened to them with pleasure, and thanked those who thus addressed him for having spoken the truth. Obedience was to him the greatest happiness. Although he was the founder and head of his order, he resigned the government of it, and declared that he was as willing to obey the youngest novice as the most ancient religious. Therefore, it is that the Church, which is the best judge of the virtue of the saints, has given him by excellence the title of " the humble." It is also in recompense of his humility that he has obtained in heaven one of the highest of those thrones of which the rebel angels were deprived in consequence of their pride.

PRAYER.

O my Saviour, it is from your instructions that St. Francis has learned this deep humility. He has advanced in it with giant strides, whilst I, a miserable sinner, overwhelmed with guilt, know not how to subdue the pride of my heart; grant me, I beseech Thee, the help of Thy Divine grace, to humble myself as I ought, and that I may never again be led astray by the spirit of pride, grant, O my God, that imitating this great saint, I may conform myself always to your divine example, and unite myself always to your cross. O glorious St. Francis, may your humility be my model, that, like you, I may desire to see myself beneath the feet of all, and that I may never forget that my true happiness consists not in earthly honours, but in suffering humiliations, and in rejoicing in them for the love of my God.

Three Our Fathers—Hail Mary, and Gloria—Hymn, versicle and prayer of the saint.

SECOND DAY.

On the poverty of St. Francis.

Evangelical poverty may be said to have been the favourite virtue of St. Francis of Assisi. When his father urged him to

It appeared to him an inestimable gift. He had asked it of God with many tears and fervent prayers. When at Rome he had addressed himself to the prince of the apostles to obtain it, and he, favourable to so holy a prayer, assured him that God had granted him this grace. He called poverty his sister, his mother, his spouse, his queen, and he always spoke of it with peculiar affection. He saw with grief the contempt and estrangement which men felt for it, and he omitted nothing to attract their hearts towards it, to win their esteem for it. If he met any one who appeared more destitute than himself, he reproached himself severely, and was filled with a holy emulation that none should surpass him in his love for his dear poverty. In a word, no one ever desired riches so ardently as he desired to be poor for the love of God.

PRAYER.

O my sweet Jesus, who can recall without the tenderest emotion the extreme poverty which Thou and Thy blessed Mother didst suffer for our sakes? It was this thought which caused Francis to weep, to meditate so constantly. As soon as he had discovered the excellence of a virtue which was so dear to you, and which you cherished in so wonderful a manner, he excited in himself such an ardent desire for it, that he could not rest without having obtained it. Ah, Lord! grant that, touched by such powerful motives, I may likewise divest myself of all ill-regulated affection for the things of earth, that I may say with truth, like my seraphic father, " Deus meus et omnia," my God is my all. O, my holy patron, obtain for me one drop of that ineffable sweetness which you found in poverty. May I no longer regard it with the eyes of blinded worldlings, but with those of your mind, that I may be touched by the powerful attractions of the most poor life of Jesus and Mary. Our Father, &c.

THIRD DAY.

The penitence of St. Francis.

One of the blessed companions of St. Francis said, that if he had been gifted as he had wished, with a stronger constitution and more robust health, no one would have exceeded him in the practice of a life of mortification and penance. Even from the first period of his conversion he observed so many lents during the year that one seemed only a continuation of that which preceded it, so that his fasts were continual. His most delicate nourishment was but a few herbs seasoned with ashes, or a little water. If during sickness he was compelled to take meat, he did penance for it as soon as the necessity of using it had ceased, and then increased his ordinary privations and added new mortifications to them. Hair-cloth disciplines, watchings, and tears were his greatest pleasure. He overcame temptations by casting himself into the snow, amongst thorns, or into the fire. He constantly sought for and found new ways of macerating his body. He had so inured himself to suffering, that the flesh was ever submissive to the spirit, so that if his will inclined him to some fresh exercise of virtue, his flesh, far from manifesting repugnance to it, seemed rather willing to aid him to fulfil his desire.

PRAYER.

O, my blessed Saviour, how different is the conduct of St. Francis to mine! He led a pure and holy life, and yet he treated himself with the greatest severity, whilst I, though overwhelmed with sin, seek only to gratify my senses, and am alarmed even at the idea of penance. O my God, may the example of Thy life, which was one continual suffering, withdraw me from this dangerous slumber, and encourage me rather to suffer a thousand deaths than to offend Thee by gratifying my passions. Such is my firm resolution, since nothing can be more contradictory than to behold a head crowned with thorns and one of its members immersed in worldly pleasures. And thou, O illustrious penitent, thou who in dying didst ask pardon of thy body for having treated it too roughly, permit not that I should so forget, through my false delicacy to mortify mine, as to be obliged to repent uselessly that I have served it but too well.

Our Father, Hail Mary, &c.

FOURTH DAY.

The patience of St. Francis.

Jesus crucified appeared to St. Francis of Assisi, and the saint in the depth of his

heart heard these words, " If you desire to
be my disciple, renounce yourself, take up
your cross, and follow me;" and immediately obeying the celestial voice, he embraced his cross with heroic patience. He
had many opportunities of bearing it in
the perfect life which he undertook. His
austerities reduced him to extreme weakness, many thought that he had lost his
reason; they reviled him; they neither
spared him insult or injury; they went so
far as even to throw stones and dirt on him,
but he went on his way as if he did not
perceive it. He bore with the same courage the ill-treatment of his father, of rob-
bers, of the Saracens, and even of the
demons. He was afflicted with various
severe and painful sicknesses. In his latter
years his emaciation was so great that he
appeared almost like a skeleton; nothing
remained but skin and bone. Nevertheless he cherished his sufferings as heavenly
gifts, and he drank the bitter chalice so
willingly that his religious were amazed
beyond measure, and believed they beheld
another Job, whose mind seemed to increase
in vigour even in proportion as his body
decayed.

PRAYER.

O my Saviour, when shall I find in the
wearinesses and sufferings of this life as
much pleasure as I now find in rest and
consolation ? In order to accomplish this
I have only to reflect on your holy Passion,
then I would adore and love your holy
will in all things ; but this is one of the
great gifts of the Holy Spirit. I ask it of
you, O my God, with the deepest humility
of heart, I am confident that you will grant
it to me, and from this hour I will return
thanks for all the afflictions that may befall
me. Alas! even should they be increased
a hundredfold, they will never exceed the
number of my sins. I will consider it a
happiness to be allowed to suffer with you,
and rejoice only in your cross. May your
sufferings, O glorious St. Francis, help to
strengthen my weakness, and to convince
me of the truth you so loved to teach ; that
the perfect joy, the true happiness and
glory of those who serve God consists in
suffering willingly for Him.

Our Father, Hail Mary, &c.

FIFTH DAY.

Charity of St. Francis of Assisi. His love of God.

St. Francis was so animated with divine love, that he resembled a seraph, it is for this reason that he is commonly called the seraphic. Whilst still young he formed a resolution never to refuse anything that was asked him for the love of God, and he observed it faithfully to the end of his life. It was this love which made him despoil himself of all that he had before the Bishop of Assisi, and led him from henceforth to live a heavenly life. It was this love which made him thrice seek the camp of the infidels, that he might shed his blood for the glory of God. This love was the motive of all that he undertook for the welfare of others. He thought he could not be the friend of God unless he laboured incessantly for the good of souls purchased by the Blood of Jesus Christ. At the very mention of the word, love of God, he was immediately inflamed with a celestial fire of this divine fire which occasioned the death of this holy patriarch.

PRAYER.

O my Saviour, the seraphic Doctor St. Bonaventura has truly said that St. Francis resembled a burning coal absorbed in the fire of your love. How confounded should I be, O my God! All creatures were so many steps by which this blessed father ascended to Thee, and furnished food for the divine love which consumed him; but as for me they are only an occasion of increased relaxation, a means of falling into sin, or of continually offending Thy Divine Majesty; vouchsafe to pardon me, O! my God; grant me, I beseech Thee, one spark of that heavenly fire which enkindled Thy blessed servant, that, following his example, I may seek only to please Thee, and consecrate myself entirely to Thy glory. And thou, O seraph of love, who excellest so exceedingly in the love of God, do not refuse me the help which I implore. Draw, by your example, all my inclinations towards this ocean of goodness, that I may henceforth fear nothing but to offend my God, and may my only consolation be to labour and suffer for His love.

SIXTH DAY.

The love of St. Francis for his neighbour.

Whoever could have penetrated into the heart of St. Francis of Assisi, would have found there a happy combination of tenderness and charity for his neighbour. While still young he gave his own clothes to a poor soldier, and often he cut or tore off part of his garments to give them to those who were in want. The service of the leper was one of his favourite occupations, he beheld in their sufferings a representation of what Christ has suffered for us. He could not even see a poor person without the tenderest pity. But the principal object of his charity was the welfare of souls. He desired to convert and sanctify the whole world, for this he neither spared himself tears or labour. He was not satisfied with employing his disciples, but gave himself up to seek for souls. With this end in view, he journeyed through many countries and kingdoms, and the vineyard of the Lord, thus watered by him, produced celestial fruit in abundance.

PRAYER.

Eternal thanks to Thee, O sweet Jesus, for all the good which the amazing charity of Francis has effected throughout the world. Alas! how far I am from imitating his blessed example. How often excessive love of self causes me to forget what I owe to others. But I repent now of my obduracy. Yes, my God, from henceforth I will see in each of my brethren another self. Since sin is the greatest evil which can befall them, deign to afflict me as it pleases Thee, but preserve them from this misfortune; for it is but just to place the salvation of souls before all things, since Thou hast given Thy life for this end. And you, O great saint, whose compassionate bounty I implore, obtain for me a heart like thine, that I may behold my neighbour, not with the prejudice of self-love, but with the sweet bond of charity which unites me to him by the profession of Christianity, and by the life and doctrine of the Saviour. Our Father, Hail Mary, &c.

SEVENTH DAY.

The devotion of St. Francis of Assisi towards the Divine Mysteries.

The ardent charity of St. Francis of Assisi, which caused him to lose all relish for the things of earth, inspired him at the same time with the most elevated sentiments for divine things. He honoured the great festivals of the Church by long lents, which consisted not merely in fasts, but in pious meditations and other exercises of his tender piety. He had a special devotion to the feast of the Nativity. One day he celebrated it with such fervour, and in so touching a manner, that all the assistants were deeply moved. Our Lord, to recompense His servant, condescended to appear to him as a little Infant lying on the crib which he had prepared.* This holy patriarch wept bitterly when he thought of the Passion of Jesus. It was his mirror, his book, and the ordinary subject of his discourse. Every one was penetrated with

---

* St. Francis was the first to institute (with the permission of the Holy See) the devotion of representing the Nativity at Christmas.

devotion when he approached to the Holy Table, and the sweetness which he experienced often ravished him into ecstasy. The greatness and virtues of the Blessed Virgin excited his admiration, and he could not think of her, nor of the angels and saints, without redoubling his love of God.

PRAYER.

It was thus, O my sweet Jesus, that St. Francis drew from Thy divine mysteries as from an inexhaustible and heavenly mine the immense treasures of perfection, and I think it a great thing if I honour them by some trifling marks of exterior devotion, even while my mind is full of a thousand follies. Ah, Lord, shed upon me the resplendent light of Thy divine countenance, that I may know Thy holy will. I adore Thee, and love Thee, in Thy life, and in Thy death; in Thy spotless Mother, and in Thy saints; but deign to show me Thy will and my duty, in order that the true spirit of your holy laws may animate my worship, and that I may offer you with my praises the sacrifice of my sinful inclinations. And thou, O most glorious Francis, perfect model of devotion, who for the glory of God rebuilt with such love so many churches falling to decay, grant me your help in order that I may myself become a living temple of the Most High, redolent with the perfume of true devotion, and that I may praise my God, not only with my words, but in my heart, by my works, and by every faculty of my being.

Our Father, Hail Mary, &c.

EIGHTH DAY.

The Stigmata or Sacred Wounds of St. Francis.

There are many points of resemblance between the life of St. Francis of Assisi, and that of our Lord Jesus Christ; but the impression of the wounds of our Divine Saviour on the body of the holy Patriarch set as it were the final seal to this resemblance. The Lord appeared to him under the form of a glorious seraphim fastened to a cross, and having by the mere apparition of his surpassing beauty, and by mysterious words of ineffable sweetness wounded his heart with love, He willed still further to wound even the flesh of His humble servant, and impressed on his hands, his feet, and his side a lively image of the wounds which He had Himself suffered on the cross for the salvation of men. This impression was accompanied with excessive pain. By the permission of the Almighty, the holy Patriarch lived for two years bearing thus in his body the precious signs of our redemption. He became a living crucifix dwelling with men, and he could say with the great apostle, " I live, but it is no longer I, it is Christ who lives in me." *Vivo ego, jàm non ego vivet verò in me Christus.*

PRAYER.

Who can worthily praise Thee, O my Saviour, for so wonderful a work. Doubtless it is not only for Francis that Thou hast accomplished it, it is for me, and for all the faithful. Thou hast willed that the wounds of Thy servant, in recalling Thine to us, should excite us to pay the debt of love which is due to Thee for Thy most bitter Passion. May Thy divine providence be for ever blest. Vouchsafe, O my God, by the merits of Thy saint, to fortify and increase the desire with which his wounds have inspired me, of dying to the world and myself, to live only for Thee, since Thou by Thy death hast become the Author of our true life. And thou, my blessed Father, inflame by the sublime ardour of your heart the joys which your wounds have caused me, in order that while embracing them with profound respect I may understand perfectly the mysterious language with which, as so many heavenly tongues, they address me : " Love your God, who by an excess of goodness has condescended to suffer and die for your love."

Our Father, Hail Mary, &c.

NINTH DAY.

The Happy Death of St. Francis.

The death of St. Francis was one of the most touching spectacles which the world has ever beheld. This glorious saint had prepared himself for it by exercises of the tenderest piety; and when his last hour arrived he remembered the abnegation of the Saviour on the cross, and would have himself placed on the bare floor to imitate his Lord. The superior then presented him with a habit saying that he gave it to him as an alms, and Francis accepted it, giving thanks to God and full of joy that he could thus die still faithful to his dear poverty. He asked to have the Passion of Christ according to St. John read to him, and then reciting himself the 141st Psalm he passed sweetly to his rest, when he had repeated the words : "Deliver, O Lord, my soul from prison, that I may praise Thy name : the just wait for me, that You may give me the recompense which You have prepared for me." Then his blessed soul was seen ascending to glory in the form of a brilliant star rising up to heaven. His body no longer appeared pale and emaciated, it became fresh and fair. The dark nails which pierced his hands and feet contracted with his wounds ; and that in the side now resembled a beautiful rose, so that those who were present were moved even to tears.

PRAYER.

O my Jesus, how precious is the death of Thy saints. When St. Francis felt his last hour approach, he returned Thee a thousand thanks, and desired that his religious should sing Thy praises. I thank Thee for this, O my God, with my whole heart, and beseech Thee by the sacred wounds of Thy servant to grant me grace henceforward to lead a new life. May I be always occupied with promoting Thy divine glory as the only interest I should have in this world, in order that my life may render my death holy, and that whether living or dying I may have the happiness of ever giving Thee glory. Such, O my blessed patron, are the holy desires which are suggested by your blessed passage from this valley of tears to our celestial country, your blessed life could not have been more happily ended. How happy shall I be if I learn to follow your example, if I feel the like sentiments in my dying hour. Far from fearing death, I will rather consider it as my benefactor and my friend; for it will deliver me from the fear of offending God, and will secure to me the happiness of loving Him eternally. May I, through your powerful intercession, obtain this grace. Amen.

Our Father, Hail Mary, &c.

HYMN,

Plaude, turba pauperoula.

Come, ye poor ones of your God,
   Come and sing your father's praise,
All his merits and his love
   Utter in melodious lays.

Simple, humble, full of peace,
   Blessings follow where he goes;
Light and joy from every word
   That he utters, richly flows.

Poverty is all he asks,
   Christ's blest wounds are in his heart,
For to poor ones our dear Lord
   Will His richest gifts impart.

Trampling down our three-fold foe,
   Thus he wins the victor's crown;
Through the world his teaching still
   Gaineth honour and renown.

Poor on earth, but rich in heaven,
   Here he wants—but golden store
He shall win who cures the souls
   And the bodies of the poor.

Father of the truly poor,
  Teach us like thyself to be ;
That with thee we may be blest,
  Rich for all eternity.

Now to Father and to Son
  And Holy Ghost be endless praise,
And may the merits of our saint
  Bring us to join angelic lays.

V. Pray for us, O blessed father St.
Francis.

R. That we may be made worthy of the
promises of Christ.

PRAYER.

O God, who, through the merits of
blessed Francis dost enlarge Thy Church by
the progeny of a new offspring ; grant unto
us, that, by imitating him, we may despise
earthly things, and ever rejoice in the
participation of heavenly gifts. Through,
&c.

NOVENA TO ST. CLARE.

FIRST DAY.

St. Clare despises all the things of earth to please Jesus Christ, and consecrates herself to her Divine Spouse before the altar of the Blessed Virgin.

St. Francis gives her the habit of the Seraphic Order.

CONSIDERATION.

There is nothing of more importance than to begin well, and to consecrate oneself early to God. Those who are so happy as to have been brought up from childhood in the fear of God usually persevere in it until death. We gather in old age what has been sown in youth; of this our saint had happy experience; from her tenderest years she applied herself to the service of God, and as she grew in years she increased in piety. Taught by the glorious patriarch St. Francis, she forsook all to take up the cross of Jesus; she left her father's house to shut herself up in the cloister; she cast off her costly apparel, for a poor and coarse habit; she cut off her hair; and at the foot of the altar of the Queen of Angels she took Jesus Christ for her Spouse, and consecrated herself to Him on the evening of Palm Sunday. The spouses of Jesus Christ are at once virgins and mothers; they are virgins by purity, mothers by the fruitfulness with which they bring forth spiritual children to the Church: *General virgo filias,* such was St. Clare. The infinite number of daughters who acknowledge her as their mother, renders her, after the mother of God, the most glorious and faithful of virgins.

COLLOQUY.

How admirable is your conduct, O eldest daughter of the patriarch of the poor. " *Quam pulchri sunt gressus tui !*" From your childhood you have continually increased in virtue, and your mind detached from earth has been only occupied with heavenly contemplation. Your shorn hair is symbolical of the contempt you entertain for all those vanities which the world esteems. O my dearest mother! how beautiful you appear to me when I behold you clothed in this serge habit, more precious in your eyes than the most costly and magnificent garment. I have chosen you for my mother, but, alas, I fear lest my infidelities to your holy rule and my attachment to earthly things will not allow you to acknowledge me for your child. Oh my holy patroness, forget my past relapses, obtain for me from your Divine Spouse, who has called me to serve Him in this monastery, the grace to follow your example and imitate your virtues. Prostrate at your feet, I implore of you with all my heart, as from the tenderest of mothers, your holy benediction. Amen.

Five Paters, Aves, and Glorias, in honour of the passion; and of the devotion of St. Clare to these mysteries.

Ant. Hail spouse of Jesus, holy virgin, little plant of the poor, vessel of singular purity; thou who hast given a rule to thy sisters, O Clare, by thy merits and prayers bring us to the celestial kingdom.

℣. Pray for us, O blessed Mother Clare,

℟. That we may be made worthy of the promises of Christ.

PRAYER.

O God, who by the admirable virtues of the blessed virgin Clare, hast adorned Thy

Church and given it new children, graciously vouchsafe, that walking in the steps of this holy virgin, we may obtain eternal joy. Through Jesus Christ our Lord.   Amen.

SECOND DAY.

St. Clare exhorts the children of a poor mother not to degenerate from her poverty;

Poverty of St. Clare.

CONSIDERATION.

The best money with which to purchase paradise is that which is drawn from the treasury of evangelical poverty.   Poverty is the hidden treasure to which Jesus Christ compares the kingdom of heaven, in St. Matthew's Gospel, and of which few indeed know the value.   The Son of God, when He came into the world, did not disdain to seek for it Himself, and the first christians, animated by His example, sold all that they had in order to purchase it. But by degrees this fervour died away.   Then God raised up St. Francis and St. Clare to manifest to all this hidden treasure, and to make it known to the world, rather by their example than by their words. O blessed poverty, for which alone the saintly Clare seems to breathe and live, thou art her inseparable companion, her mother, her beloved sister, her constant thought, her heart's delight. When elected Abbess she built her first monastery on the foundation of extreme poverty; she and her children would subsist only on alms, and when the Sovereign Pontiff wished to dispense her from this vow of poverty which appeared too rigorous, she replied quickly, that if he wished to confer a favour on her, she begged he would absolve her from her sins, rather than dispense her from a vow in which she found so much happiness. Oh! how secure we are when we make ourselves poor for the love of God like St. Clare, and when we place all our confidence in God. Oh! how they should tremble for their salvation who despise the vow of poverty which they have made.

COLLOQUY.

fully. And that I may not degenerate from that rigid poverty which you so often inculcated on your dear children, I am firmly resolved not only to abandon all superfluities, but even to repress the least desire of possessing them, because I am convinced, like St. Teresa, that a religious cannot be considered truly poor who has every necessary. I desire, then, for the love of God, to suffer all the inconvenience of poverty even in necessary things, choosing always that which is the poorest, the most useless, and the most painful to self-love. The poorer a religious is in this life, the richer her Divine Spouse will make her after death. We are truly rich even if deprived of all things, if we possess Jesus Christ; we are poor in the midst of riches if we have not Jesus.

Pater, Ave, &c.

THIRD DAY.

St. Clare hears with the utmost attention the words of wisdom when the preacher of grace declares the words of life.

Humility of St. Clare.

CONSIDERATION.

Humility is the most important lesson which we have to learn in the school of Jesus Christ. "Learn of Me, for I am meek and humble of heart." One act of humility is worth infinitely more than all the learning in the world. He who wishes to acquire the virtues of Christianity without having humility for a foundation, is like the foolish architect who built his house upon the shifting sands. It was not thus St. Clare acted. Attentive to the words of divine wisdom, which promise salvation to the humble soul, and supported by the instructions of St. Francis, she was humble in her thoughts, in her desires, in her words, in her actions, in all her conduct. For three years she persisted in refusing the dignity of abbess. And when at length she yielded in obedience, she only used her

authority as a means of humbling herself
more. She would stand while the other
religious were seated, and offer them water
to wash their hands, or wash and kiss their
feet. The great esteem in which she was
held by the Sovereign Pontiffs, far from
exciting thoughts of pride, served her rather
as an occasion of humility. It was thus
that she made herself continually more
worthy of the graces which the Lord bestowed on her; for as pride is the source
of every evil, so is humility the source of
all good.

COLLOQUY.

Oh, how beautiful thou art, holy mother,
adorned in heaven with the rich and brilliant crown won by your humility. If
when on earth you never refused the lowest
offices, if acts of humility were your delight,
it was because you knew that those who
humble themselves on earth shall be exalted in heaven, " *qui se humiliat, exalta-
bitur.*" Make one ray of this precious
virtue shine upon me. Do not permit that
one who wears your humble habit should
retain in her heart the least thought of
pride. Make my interior sentiments cor-
respond faithfully with the lowliness of the

garment which I wear. Knowing that I am a sinner and a nothing, I desire by your example to humble myself with my whole heart for the love of Jesus Christ, who has humbled Himself to death, even to the death of the cross. I desire to bear all the injuries and contempt which may be shown to me, and as holy obedience is the inseparable companion of humility, I promise to obey blindly and to submit with a willing mind to all that I am commanded to do, that, like you, I may attain one day to the glory which God has prepared for the humble.

Pater, Ave, &c.

FOURTH DAY.

The little plant of St. Francis produces wonderful fruit through the whole world, and innumerable virgins are trained in the school of St. Clare.

Virginal purity of St. Clare.

CONSIDERATION.

The care of a skilful gardener is necessary in order to make a plant increase and bear fruit, and such was the blessed Patriarch Francis in regard to our holy mother, manifesting to her the designs which he had formed for her. Mystical plant transplanted into the cloister of St. Damiens, what sweet odours you will soon spread abroad, what numbers of holy daughters, following your example, will flock hither to consecrate themselves to God by a solemn vow of chastity. But further, O wise virgin, with what care will you not encourage them to preserve scrupulously this treasure of poverty which makes us even like to God. It is for this that holy virgins are compared to the angels in paradise, and that these blessed spirits almost envy their lot. For, says St. Bernard, the angels live virgins, but they have not a body continually weighing them down to earth, whilst virgins are exposed to a continual combat with the senses. The angels are indeed happier, but virgins are more admirable. It is on this account that St. Ambrose says that virginity is not to be praised because it is found in the martyrs, but rather because it makes martyrs of all those who combat generously to preserve it. Oh, how great, exclaimed St. Clare to her daughters, how great is the recompense which God has prepared in heaven for chaste souls. Let us strive to merit it.

COLLOQUY.

I salute you, faithful spouse of Jesus Christ, sacred virgin, seraphic plant, beneath whose shadow so many lilies, radiant with purity, have flourished even ' to our own days. Your holy lessons recall the recompense which is prepared for pure virgins. Nevertheless I tremble when I think of the fearful pains, the eternal torments which await those spouses who are unfaithful to their sacred engagements. Drive away, I beseech you, all that may impress my senses. Turn away my eyes from the vanities of the earth. " *Averte oculos meos ne videant vanitatem.*" Far from me be all sensual pleasures, all thoughts, all dangerous conversations which might make me lose the treasures of eternity. I purpose, with the help of divine grace, to watch and combat without ceasing, that I may not lose the crown of virgins and may win the crown of martyrs.

Pater, Ave, &c.

FIFTH DAY.

St. Clare, walking with fervour in the path of penance, marks out for us the way which leads to heaven.

The Penance of St. Clare.

CONSIDERATION.

There is no surer presage, no more unfailing sign of great sanctity than patience in sufferings, and love of mortification. To arrive at the celestial Jerusalem, it is not sufficient to lead a pure life and one exempt from great faults, we must also, according to the example of St. Paul, chastise our bodies and reduce them to obedience, *" Castigo corpus meum et in servitutem redigo."* Convinced of this truth, St. Clare, notwithstanding the purity and innocence of her life, ceased not to afflict and torment her body, to render herself more pleasing and more conformable to Jesus crucified. While still in the world she always wore a cilice under her costly attire, and deprived herself with joy of every delicacy to bestow it secretly on the poor. When a religious, she only wore a woollen tunic of the coarsest material, and covered with patches. Her feet were bare; her bed vine leaves; her pillow a block of wood. In memory of the stripes and wounds of her Blessed Master, she wore a coarse cord with thirteen knots, and a cilice of horse-hair so heavy and painful, that one of the most robust amongst her sisters could scarcely bear it for three days. Her ordinary food was herbs or vegetables, but during Lent and Advent she took only bread and water, and even of this she deprived herself each Monday, Wednesday, and Friday. For fifty-eight years she bore the greatest sufferings with perfect tranquillity, knowing that the most blessed days of our lives are those on which God deigns to visit us with some suffering. Thus live those happy souls who are filled with divine love, the faithful spouses of Jesus Christ.

COLLOQUY.

How confounded I am, oh! my holy mother, when I consider the severity of your penance. Though your soul was pure and innocent, and you were loaded with the benedictions of heaven, you ceased not to afflict and crucify your flesh as if you had been the greatest sinner in the world. And even when it was already worn out by long vigils, and seemed no longer capable of rebelling against you, you ceased not to mortify it by fasts, by hair-cloths, and the most rigorous austerities. And I, miserable though I am, full of vices and imperfections, have a horror of penance. You continually implored your Lord for sufferings, and I, on the contrary, almost desire that He should work miracles to deliver me from the most trifling affliction. Oh, what a rigorous account I will have to render to God at the moment of my death if I do not seriously enter into myself. But I am resolved, with the help of Divine grace, to bear the cross of penance courageously, to repress the perverse inclinations of nature, and to expiate by mortification the sins and errors of my life. Penance closes the gates of hell and opens those of paradise. Oh, hell, how fearful thou art! oh, paradise, how sweet!

Oh, holy mother, deliver me from the one, and obtain for me, through the divine mercy, entrance into the other.

Pater, Ave, &c.

SIXTH DAY.

St. Clare, a true lover of the cross, teaches her children to mourn for Jesus crucified, and weeps for Him also herself.

Devotion of St. Clare to the Passion of Jesus Christ.

CONSIDERATION.

The good example of superiors is a source of the greatest blessing, and when combined with their charitable instructions, it produces the most beneficent results in regard to those under their guidance. When the Spirit of God animates those who govern a community, we soon see abundant fruit. All who associated with Clare felt the benefit of her sanctity. To excite her novices to virtue, she gave them the example of it. A true lover of the cross, she often ascended the hill of Calvary, and there, pouring forth her tears, she exhorted her children to draw the salutary waters of grace from the wounds of their Saviour. Often she was transported in spirit to the garden of Gethsemani, and there she would make for herself a bundle of myrrh, mingling her tears with the bloody sweat of her suffering Jesus. In the pretorium of Pilate she contemplated the pure flesh of Jesus torn by the scourges, and His head crowned with thorns, and this wounded her inmost heart. All the instruments of the Passion of Jesus penetrated her with the most lively grief. The cross of the Redeemer was the ordinary subject of her conversations. She knew that it was the golden book where the souls predestined by the blood of Jesus Christ are registered, and that the most sublime science is to know Jesus, and Jesus crucified. "Non enim predicavi," she would say with the apostle, "me scire aliquid vitu vos nisi Jesum Christum, et hunc crucifixum."

COLLOQUY.

Teach me to weep, oh dear tears of St. Clare, teach me to weep for the Passion of my Saviour; impress on my heart this salutary lesson; that he who desires to have a share in the kingdom of heaven, must partake with Jesus in the sorrows of Calvary. He who walks on this road will find continual triumphs, while he who seeks another will encounter only defeat. I desire then, by your example, O my blessed mother, to ascend the mountain of myrrh. There, I will learn, like you, that in order to be transfigured with Jesus on Thabor, we must be transpierced with Him on Calvary. Obtain for me, I implore you, from this dear Jesus whom you have so ardently loved, that He will come and dwell in my heart, and that His sacred wounds may close it to all besides; that the nails which pierced His hands and feet may bind me for ever to His cross, so that my thoughts and my desires may never more wander from my crucified Redeemer; that the thorns which pierced His Heart may pierce my heart, so as to close it against all the temptations of the evil one; that the gall with which His lips were moistened may flow upon even the innocent joys of my life. If I have this happiness, blessed mother, I may truly reckon myself amongst the number of your children.

Pater, Ave, &c.

SEVENTH DAY.

St. Clare delivers her fellow citizens by her prayers, and drives from her monastery the barbarians who threaten it.

Devotion of St. Clare towards the most Holy Sacrament.

CONSIDERATION.

Devotion towards the most Holy Sacrament is a furnace which has always enkindled and inflamed the hearts of saints; it is the fountain of life from which they drew those celestial streams which watered their souls, and brought forth fruit in them unto life eternal. Strengthened by this divine nourishment, they resisted all the temptations of hell, and even ceased to care for the pleasures of earth. St. Clare, from her earliest years, entertained so profound a veneration for the most Holy Sacrament, that all her desire was to frequent the churches, there to adore her Lord. She passed many hours of the day, and often a great part of the night, before the tabernacle, occupied in sweet converse with Jesus Christ, hidden under the sacramental species.

When her infirmity hindered her from visiting Him thus, she employed her time in spinning thread for linen, of which she made corporals for poor churches. When she approached the holy table she shed such abundant tears that her countenance appeared inflamed. When she reflected on her own nothingness, and the greatness of Him whom she was about to receive into her heart, she was filled with a holy ravishment. What humility, what devotion! we may well ask, was there ever any greater than that of St. Clare? But what miracles also! Assisi is besieged by the Saracens, and the barbarians have already scaled the walls of St. Damiens. At the same moment, forgetful of her own infirmities, she causes herself to be carried with the most Holy Sacrament to the gate of the monastery. She prays, and then she hears a divine voice which utters these words, " I will preserve you for ever." Again she prays, and the same voice assures her that Assisi will be delivered. She displays the ciborium to the infidels, and in an instant the place is free, the town is saved, and the spouses of Jesus have nothing more to fear.

4

COLLOQUY.

O holy mother, I am filled with compunction on considering all that you did before venturing to refresh yourself with the Body and Blood of Jesus Christ in the sacrament of the Eucharist. Alas! where are my tears? Where are my sighs? Where is the ardour which should inflame me when I approach the holy communion? O my soul, soul insensible to the benefits of God, why dost thou not fear? Why dost thou not weep? Why dost thou not burn with love like the blessed Clare? It is because thou art full of pride. Destitute of virtue, thou dost not reflect sufficiently on thy misery, or thy unworthiness, and on the majesty of the God whom thou art about to entertain. What union can exist between the Body of Jesus mortified, of Jesus crucified, and one who is nothing but sensuality and self-love? This sacrament is the memorial of His Passion, and thou dreadest suffering. This is a sacrament of love, since it has its origin in love, and it produces love in the soul that receives it, and thou comest to, and goest from, this burning furnace colder than ice. What insensibility! what ingratitude!

what a subject of confusion, what a motive for grief and repentance. Oh holy mother, I acknowledge myself unworthy to be reckoned amongst the number of your children, and still more to be nourished with the bread of angels. But since my good Jesus has commanded me to approach to His holy table, and that He even threatens me with His anger if I refuse to eat His Flesh and drink His Blood, I will approach for the future with the greatest confidence, and the most profound respect, I will receive Him into my heart that He may expel the enemy of my salvation; and then, following your example, I will sing the mercies of my Divine Liberator.

Pater, Ave, &c.

EIGHTH DAY.

St. Francis of Assisi, the servant of God, excites St. Clare to love the God whose love has made Him become man.

Love of St. Clare for God.

CONSIDERATION.

Love can only work great things. If it

is profane, it makes great sinners ; if it is divine it makes great saints. A thousand times blessed are they who burn with the same fire as St. Clare. The inhabitants of heaven are happy only because they possess it, and if the Divine Will enabled the lost to produce one act of the love of God, this single act would suffice to extinguish the flames of hell in an instant. Let us consider the wonderful effects produced in the heart of St. Clare by those celestial flames. Let us glance over her life, and we shall see that it was a continual martyrdom of love. This was the soul of all her virtues, the foundation of her merit, and the fundamental motive of her great penance. What a thirst to hear the word of God! what ardent desires to fly to the country of the infidel that she might obtain the martyr's palm! The ravishments and ecstasies which she experienced when God was spoken of, were the exterior proofs of what passed in her soul. She continually exhorted her children to use every effort to merit the gift of Divine Love. She taught them the means to acquire it, namely, detachment from creatures, privation of earthly pleasures, mortification of the senses, silence of the heart, and victory over their passions.

They who live thus, following the example of St. Clare, will find Jesus, will love Jesus, will live in the Heart of Jesus, and Jesus will live in theirs. *Qui manet in charitate, in Deo manet et Deus in eo.*

COLLOQUY.

Although I do not merit your favours, O blessed mother, yet I beseech you hear my prayer, obtain for me, I implore you, one spark of that tender love, so constant and so generous, which made you so ardently desire the glory of God. This little spark will be sufficient, by purifying me more and more from my sins, to give me strength to resist courageously all the attacks of the evil one. This divine light will show me the value of the grace which was conferred on me, in bringing me to serve God in this monastery. I am confounded to see how negligent I have been in corresponding to so singular a favour. " *Charitatem primam dereliquisti.*" Thou hast forsaken thy first love. Yes, it is to me that this terrible reproach is addressed. I have lost, through my own fault, my first fervour. I have gone back instead of advancing in the service and love of God. For how have I used the many holy inspirations, the many

special graces which I have received from
God? What fruit have I gained from the
many good examples I constantly see; from
so many pious lectures, so many retreats,
meditations, and still more from the many
sacraments I have received? Grant me
your blessed protection, O my good mother,
that I may again enter on the path of
divine love. Teach me how to serve my
God well, that I may love Him well.
Make me understand, and engrave deeply
on my heart this truth, that a love which
does not seek Jesus with ardour in every-
thing, is weak, languishing, and imperfect.
Oh, how happy, how rich I should be, if my
heart was full of the love of Jesus Christ,
how perfect I should be if in all my actions
I only sought to please Jesus. We must
love Him on earth, if we would one day
possess Him in heaven.

Pater, Ave, &c.

NINTH DAY.

After a holy life full of merit the soul of St. Clare ascends to heaven, accompanied by a troop of Virgins.

St. Clare passes from earth to heaven.

CONSIDERATION.

How sweet is death to a soul which has passed its life in the service of God! No, it is not terrible for one who has lived piously ; on the contrary it is the object of her desires, because she regards it as the termination of her combats, and the commencement of her happiness. Of this the Blessed virgin Clare furnishes us with a proof. Having passed forty-two years in the service of God, she beheld the approach of her last hour with the greatest confidence and the most perfect security. She exhorted her soul to leave her body, to enjoy end." At this moment the Blessed Virgin Mary appeared in her poor cell, surrounded by a troop of virgins. She approached her bed, embraced her tenderly, and then conducted her soul to the abode of the blest. Thus do the just die, if indeed we may call that death which is the commencement of unending life. God never forsakes those in their last moments who have served Him faithfully in life. On the, contrary, He sustains and strengthens them by the aid of His grace, He makes them rest on His bosom; He commands His angels to defend them, to receive their souls and to bear them up to heaven, even as He did for the Blessed Clare.

COLLOQUY.

O my blessed mother, my soul is full of joy, when I consider your passage from this life of misery to your heavenly country. The poor garment which served to protect your mortal body from the rigours of the season is now changed into a mantle of glory surpassing the riches of Solomon; your humility has purchased heaven; your poverty has put you in possession of the treasures of paradise; the modesty which you so scrupulously observed has merited for you the crown of virgins; the austerity of your penance has opened a path for you strewn with roses and lilies; the attention with which you meditated all your life on the Passion of your Redeemer, has procured for you the happiness of enjoying His resurrection glory for all eternity. You now taste, and will taste for ever, the hidden manna which contains all the sweetness of heaven, in recompense of the profound veneration which you had for the Most Holy Sacrament. In fine, your ardent charity has exalted you amongst the seraphim to possess and contemplate eternally that God, who was ever the object of your love. But the more I rejoice in your unending glory, the more I am troubled and overwhelmed by my own misery. To die a holy death like yours, I feel that I must live a holy life. I need your powerful assistance to accomplish this. The love which you entertained for your children while on earth has not lessened now that you are in heaven. Obtain for me of my profession. Accept, I implore you, these little devotions which I now conclude, and obtain notwithstanding my coldness, that they may be for my eternal welfare, that they may renew in me the love of God, the love of my neighbour, and that spirit of mortification which is so essential for me. In fine, O my glorious Mother, do not abandon me at the awful moment of death, obtain for me the last grace, the grace of final perseverance; obtain for me the grace to resign my soul into the hands of my Creator, kissing tenderly the wounds of my Saviour, and uttering the holy names of Jesus and Mary; and since before thy death thou didst bless all thy children present and to come, I beseech of you now to pour down your special benediction on me and on every member of this Community.

Pater, Ave, &c.

HYMN.

Concinat plebs Fidelium.

That happy Virgin let us sing,
   Who follows in the train
Of Christ's blest Mother, and for Him
   New spouses still doth gain.

Of poverty the first-born plant,
   Rich in celestial grace;
With those who all for God have left
   She finds her blessed place.

And pouring floods of light around,
   Justly her name is Clare,
For the Eternal Light hath willed,
   That she new light should bear.

Her infant heart to Christ her Lord
   With tenderest love is given,
Till following Francis, she becomes
   The happy bride of Heaven.

Then spurning all that men count dear,
   Prizing what men call loss;
She follows Mary, and with her,
   She stands beneath the cross.

No longer worldly pomp allures,
  Nor wealth, nor noble birth ;
And in her happy cloistered home
  She thinks no more of earth.

There in love's prison sweetly bound
  She has but one desire,
To praise her Lord each day still more,
  To love with deeper fire.

Oh blessed prison, where her soul
  Alone can roam at will,
Where every hour to Christ her Lord
  She is yet dearer still.

There poorly clad, in fast and prayer,
  She rests not day or night
From holy toil, to win the crown
  Of everlasting light.

May her blest merits to the great
  Co-equal Three give praise,
To Father, Son, and Holy Ghost
  Through never ending days.

NOVENA FOR THE FEAST OF THE STIGMATA, SEPTEMBER 17TH.

FIRST DAY.

O sweet Jesus, who hast Thyself taught us to be meek and humble of heart, I offer Thee Thy own deep humility, and in union with it, the humility of St. Francis, in reparation for all my sins of pride, and to obtain grace from henceforth to practise the most profound humility in my every thought, word, and action.

Five Gloria Patris in honour of the wounds of Jesus, and the sacred Stigmata of St. Francis.

SECOND DAY.

O sweet Jesus, who for our love wast born poor, of a poor mother, in a poor stable, and who hast so singularly loved and honoured poverty; I offer Thee Thy own most blessed poverty, and in union with it the holy poverty of St. Francis, praying, that like him I too may become truly poor, and henceforth desire nothing but to be poor with Thee on earth, that I may be rich with Thee in heaven.

Five Gloria Patris, &c.

THIRD DAY.

O sweet Jesus, who for our sake didst so often fast and watch in prayer, I offer Thee all Thy blessed fastings and watchings; and in union with them the constant fasts and great austerities of the blessed Francis, praying that through his merits I may obtain grace henceforth so to mortify my body on earth, and to conquer my miserable self-love, that I may daily become more fervent and devoted in Thy divine service.

Five Gloria Patris, &c.

FOURTH DAY.

O sweet Jesus, who didst bear with such exceeding patience all the trials and distresses of our mortal life, I humbly offer Thee Thine own adorable patience; and in union with it the great patience with which St. Francis supported so many sicknesses and trials, praying that through his merits I may obtain the grace of patience, and glorify Thee by bearing meekly all the little trials and annoyances of my daily life.

Five Gloria Patris, &c.

FIFTH DAY.

O sweetest Jesus, who hast loved us so much, and who art loved so little by us, I rejoice in the great love which the blessed Francis had for Thee, and I humbly pray Thee by his merits, for the sake of Thine own inconceivable love, to kindle in my heart such an ardent fire of charity, that henceforth I may be entirely consumed with love, and have no other thought or desire but to please Thee.

Five Gloria Patris, &c.

SIXTH DAY.

O sweetest Jesus, who didst so tenderly love Thy own Immaculate Mother, and dying didst give *her* to us that we might honour and cherish her, and *us* to her that she might be our very own Mother; I offer Thee the tender love which St. Francis entertained for her, and the ardent desire he had that all men should honour her, particularly in the mystery of her Immaculate Conception, and I pray, sweet Jesus, by Thy love for Mary, and the merits of Francis, that I may ever increase in fervent devotion to Thy blessed mother, and may never say, or do, anything that would be in the least displeasing to her dear and adorable Heart.

Five Gloria Patris, &c.

SEVENTH DAY.

O sweet Lord Jesus, who wast obedient at Nazareth to Mary and Joseph, and on the cross to Thy cruel executioners, I offer Thee the deep obedience of the blessed Francis to Thy holy will, to his ecclesiastical superiors, and to all creatures for Thy sake ; and I pray that through his merits I may obtain the grace of a prompt, cheerful, and loving obedience to those whom Thou hast placed over me, and that Thou wouldst grant to them the special graces and consolations they need for their holy office.

Five Gloria Patris.

EIGHTH DAY.

Oh sweet Jesus, Good Samaritan, who wert so full of the tenderest charity for all Thy creatures, I offer Thee the devotion with which St. Francis nursed the lepers and consoled the sick, the great love which he had for his spiritual children, and his unwearied zeal for the welfare of all mankind; by Thy own ineffable charity towards poor sinners, and through the merits of Francis I humbly pray for the grace of a most tender and self-sacrificing charity towards all men, and that I may exercise it specially towards those with whom I live.

Five Gloria Patris, as above.

NINTH DAY.

O sweet Jesus, whose most bitter Passion is so little thought of, and so little loved, I rejoice in the great tenderness that the blessed Francis felt for it, and the tears he shed over Thy sufferings; O sweet Jesus, for the sake of Thy most bitter and cruel Passion, and for the great merits of Francis, which obtained for him the favour of the impression of Thy most sacred wounds,

grant me grace so to love and compassionate
Thy sufferings that I may be incited to a
continual reparation for them, and to an
ever increased devotion to the adorable
Sacrament of the altar ; and may so weep
with Thee here, that I may be made
worthy to rejoice with Thee eternally in
heaven.

Five Gloria Patris, as above.

PRAYER TO ST. FRANCIS OF ASSISI.*

O seraphic Francis! who art now in
possession of that seat among the seraphim,
which from all eternity was prepared for
thee, vouchsafe we beseech thee to join us,
while we thank thy Divine Benefactor for
having chosen thee to be the companion of
His cross, and the peculiar object of His
love. We most confidently present to thee
all our present petitions, convinced that
thy influence in heaven must be great,
since thy likeness to Jesus Christ secured
the success of thy prayers even on earth.
Thou didst early burst every human tie,
and disdain any father but God. Penetrated with the great truths of faith, thou

didst trample on all that the world calls
delightful and valuable, and didst embrace
such destitute poverty, and austere penance
as soon likened thee to that Man of Sorrows,
who had not whereon to lay His Sacred
Head. The cross of Jesus became Thy
delight, thy only treasure; and intimate
union with its adorable Victim was the only
joy thy pure soul could value. At length,
the sword of mortification opened for thee
a passage to the Heart of Jesus, the most
profound humility introduced thee into the
inmost recesses of that sacred sanctuary, the
gift of sublime prayer disclosed to thee
such transporting beauties in Jesus, that
every human object disappeared from
thine eyes. Jesus became truly "thy
God and thy All." The ardour of thy
love rendered thy whole being a burning
holocaust; and thy body itself, purified and
subdued, was honoured with the most
precious of all favours, the sacred marks of
thy Redeemer's wounds. From that happy
moment the remainder of thy banishment
was a martyrdom of love, until love itself
put an end to thy mortal life. O seraph of
the earth! have compassion on our tepidity.
Heavenly contemplative enlighten our dark-
ness. remember that the blindness of

sinners often drew tears from thy eyes.
Thou didst unceasingly lament that Jesus
should have endured such torments, and
yet that no one thought of His sufferings.
Thou canst now satisfy thy ardent desire of
seeing Jesus loved by obtaining for us the
most generous and perfect love of God, the
most profound and practical humility, a
sincere love of poverty, lively zeal for our
own perfection, and that of others, the
pirit of prayer founded on, and nourished
by universal mortification, and the particu-
ar intentions of this novena.

LITANY OF ST. FRANCIS OF ASSISI.

Lord, have mercy on us.
Christ, have mercy on us.
Lord, have mercy on us.
Christ, hear us.
Christ, graciously hear us.
God, the Father of heaven, *have mercy on us.*
God, the Son, Redeemer of the world, *have
mercy on us.*
God, the Holy Ghost, *have mercy on us.*
Holy Trinity one God, *have mercy on us.*
Holy Mary, *pray for us.*
Patroness of the Seraphic Order, *pray for
us.*

St. Francis,

St. Francis, an angel in purity,

St. Francis, ardent lover of poverty,

St. Francis, perfectly despising the world,

St. Francis, wonderful example of penance,

St. Francis, fervent imitator of your crucified Saviour,

St. Francis, bearing the stigmata of Christ,

St. Francis, a seraph by the ardour of your love,

St. Francis, profoundly humble,

St. Francis, pillar of the Church, and defender of the Faith,

St. Francis, who lived and died in transports of love,

Pray for us.

Lamb of God, who takest away the sins of the world,

Spare us, O Lord.

Lamb of God, who takest away the sins of the world,

Hear us, O Lord.

Lamb of God, who takest away the sins of the world,

Have mercy upon us, O Lord,

℣. Pray for us, O glorious St. Francis,
℟. That we may be made worthy of the promises of Christ.

Let us pray.

O God, who by the merits of St. Francis, didst increase the Church with a new progeny, grant us, by his imitation, to despise earthly things, and for ever to partake of heavenly graces, through Jesus Christ our Lord.   Amen.

———

PRAYER TO ST. CLARE.

O Divine Jesus, the Spouse of virgins, and eternal rewarder of those who are so happy as to leave all on earth, that they may find all in heaven, look down we beseech Thee on us with eyes of mercy. We assemble here to thank Thee for the favours bestowed on our blessed Foundress and Patroness St. Clare, to acknowledge how deeply we are indebted to Thy eternal predilection for being ranked among her children, and to implore through Thy compassionate heart, and her intercession, the intentions of this Novena. And thou, O illustrious patroness of Poor Clares! Seraphic spouse of the Sacred Heart of Jesus in the sacrament of His love; thou didst early select that adorable sanctuary for thy refuge and dwelling. There thy angelic soul was perfectly purified, there thou wert enriched by a sublime gift of heavenly contemplation. In that furnace of eternal love where thy merit was consummated and all thy sacrifices rewarded, thou didst enjoy an anticipated paradise. O holy Mother St. Clare, thou knowest by thy own happy experience, that it is sweet to serve God, despising this world; deign then to consider and provide for the spiritual and temporal wants of every member of this Community. May we all not alone bear thy name, but imitate thy virtues. Obtain for us that holy spirit of poverty for which thou wert so signally distinguished, and which detached thee from all things created; that perfect obedience which left thee no will but the will of thy crucified Spouse; and an ardent devotion to the adorable sacrament of the altar.

We recommend to thee also the poor children committed to our care, deign to take them under thy protection, to preserve them from the dangers of the world, and grant that being one day associated to thy blessed company. we may be also followed by those

whom we have here endeavoured to impress with the love and fear of their
Creator.   Amen.

LITANY OF ST. CLARE.

Lord, have mercy on us.
Christ, have mercy on us.
Lord, have mercy on us.
God, the Father of heaven, *have mercy on us.*
Holy Mary, Mother of God,
Holy Mary, patroness of the Seraphic
   Order,
Holy Mother Clare,
Virgin, disciple of the Mother of
   Jesus,
Virgin, first plant of the poor,
Virgin, fervent follower of our holy
   Father St. Francis,
Seraphical Virgin,
Virgin, hidden from the world,
Virgin, lily of chastity,
Virgin, lover of poverty,
Virgin, rose of penance,
Virgin, following the Lamb whitherso-
   ever He goeth,
Virgin, terror of infidels,
Virgin, burning with love to Jesus
   crucified,

Pray for us.

Virgin, enlightened by the Eternal Light,

Virgin, whose name is light,

Virgin, model of religious perfection,

Virgin, devout lover of Jesus in the Sacrament of Love,

Virgin, devoted to prayer and penance,

Lamb of God, &c.

℣. Pray for us, O blessed Mother Clare,

℞. That we may be made worthy of the promises of Christ.

Let us pray.

Grant, O Lord, we beseech Thee, that we Thy servants commemorating the votive commemoration of Thy Virgin, and our blessed Mother Clare, may, through her intercession, be partakers of celestial joys and co-heirs of Thy only begotten Son our Lord Jesus Christ. Amen.

———

A PRAYER TO ST. FRANCIS AND ST. CLARE, FOR PERSONS LIVING IN THE WORLD.

O glorious saint, ardent lover of Jesus crucified, obtain for me the grace of a burning love to my crucified Saviour, and

an earnest desire to imitate thy fervent
devotion. Thou knowest, O great saint,
to how many dangers and temptations I
am exposed, and that I may need thy
powerful protection even more than those
favoured souls who serve God in the
cloister; but though I may have less
claim upon thee, I believe thy charity to be
so great that thou wilt compassionate my
necessities and abundantly succour me.
Obtain for me the grace to sanctify all the
duties of my state of life by performing
them purely for God alone, that I may
never forget my last end, and the great
duty of preparing for it. I offer thy burning
love to God in reparation for my coldness
and indifference in His service, and I pray
that as His blessed wounds were imprinted
upon Thy hands and feet and side, so I
may ever have in my heart a constant
remembrance of the sufferings of Jesus,
as a motive to increase my love of
Him, and my dread of ever offending
Him.

Our Father, Hail Mary, and Gloria
Patri for the increase and sanctification of
the Franciscan Order, and that you may
have a share in the prayers and merits of the
many fervent souls who serve God in it,

also in thanksgiving for the graces bestowed on them.

TO ST. CLARE.

O blessed saint, who didst give thyself so early to Jesus, grant that I may imitate thy blessed example, as far as my state in life will permit, and that I may never prove a hindrance, either in word or deed, to any who desire to consecrate themselves to God, as you did. Oh! dear saint, whose very name is light, and whose heart was ever full of such tender love to Jesus crucified, obtain for me the grace of Divine light and guidance in all my undertakings, and of such ardent love of my adorable Saviour that I may be willing, nay rather that I may prefer to endure any suffering sooner than offend Him, even by a wilful imperfection. And as thou wast conducted to heaven by the Blessed and Immaculate Mother of God, oh! intercede with her for me that I may so love and serve her in life as to be worthy to be received into her maternal arms in the hour of my death, and to be presented by her to Jesus. Amen.

PRAYERS IN HONOUR OF THE FIVE WOUNDS OF OUR LORD JESUS CHRIST; COMPOSED BY ST. CLARE.

TO THE WOUND OF THE RIGHT HAND.

All praise, honour, and glory be to Thee, O Lord Jesus, for the most sacred wound of Thy right hand. By this most holy wound pardon me, I beseech Thee, the sins which I have committed against Thee, in thought, word, or deed; and the sensualities of which sleeping or waking I may have been guilty. Grant that I may ever have before me a pious remembrance of Thy wounds, and that I may testify my gratitude to Thee for having received them, by imprinting them on my own body through a continual mortification. Deign to grant this, O Lord, who livest and reignest for ever and ever. Amen.
Pater, Ave.

TO THE WOUND OF THE LEFT HAND.

All praise, honour, and glory be to Thee, O sweetest Jesus, for the most holy wound of Thy left hand. By this sacred wound show mercy unto me, and take from my heart all that is displeasing to Thee. Make me victorious over the enemies that cease not to war against me; grant me Thy strength and power that I may trample them beneath my feet. By Thy holy death deliver me from all the dangers to which my life and salvation are exposed, and render me worthy to partake of Thy glory in Thy heavenly kingdom, world without end. Amen.

Pater, Ave.

TO THE WOUND OF THE RIGHT FOOT.

All praise, honour, and glory be to Thee, O good Saviour Jesus, for the sacred wound of Thy right foot. By this most holy wound grant me to merit forgiveness from Thee, by a penance proportioned to the enormity of my sins; oh! by Thy most holy Passion, grant that my will may be ever united to Thine, and defend my body and soul from all adversity. When the day of awful judgment shall be at hand, deign mercifully to receive my soul, and make it a possessor of Thy eternal joys, O Thou who livest for ever and ever. Amen.

Pater, Ave.

TO THE WOUND OF THE LEFT FOOT.

All praise, honour, and glory be to Thee, O most merciful Jesus, for the sacred wound of Thy left foot. By this most holy wound I beg of Thee to grant me the full and entire remission of all my sins, that I may escape the rigours of Thy dread judgment. O most merciful Jesus, I implore, by your holy death, that before mine I may worthily receive the sacrament of Thy Body and Blood, that I may be able to confess all my sins, with perfect contrition and great purity of body and soul; and that I may receive the sacrament of Extreme Unction to my eternal salvation. Grant this I beseech Thee, O Lord, who livest and reignest for ever and ever. Amen.

Pater, Ave.

TO THE WOUND OF THE SIDE.

All praise, honour, and glory be to Thee, O loving Jesus, for the sacred wound of Thy side. I beg of Thee, by this most holy wound, and by the charity Thou didst show in allowing Thy most Sacred Heart to be laid open to us by the lance of the soldier Longinus, that Thou wouldest deign not only to purify me from original sin by baptism, but also to deliver me from all evils, past, present, and to come, by the merits of Thy Precious Blood, which is at this moment offered and received throughout the world. Through Thy bitter death grant me a lively faith, a firm hope, and a perfect contrition, that I may love Thee with all my heart, with all my soul, and with all my strength. Confirm me in good works, that I may persevere with courage in Thy holy service, so that I may be found pleasing in Thy divine sight, now and evermore. Amen.

Pater Ave.

℣. We adore Thee, O Christ, and we bless Thee,

℞. Because by Thy death and by Thy blood, Thou hast redeemed the world.

PRAYER.

Almighty and eternal God, who hast redeemed the world by the five wounds of Thy Son our Lord Jesus Christ, grant we beseech Thee, that we who daily honour those wounds, may be delivered from sudden and eternal death. This we implore through the same Lord Jesus, who liveth and reigneth with Thee for ever and ever.

NOVENA TO ST. COLETTE.*

FIRST DAY.

On the End of Man.

Consider why you have been placed in this world? It is only that you may love, reverence, and serve God, and by so doing save your soul.

Consider again why God has made all that exists; why He permits all that happens? It is in order to assist us to attain the end for which He has created us. From this it follows that there is only one thing necessary for you, and this one thing is to save your soul. Nothing which exists, which you see, which happens to you, is of

---

* The feast of St. Colette occurs on the 6th March. She belonged to the Order of Poor Clares, and founded many convents, whose religious are called from her Poor Clare Colettines. It is hoped this novena may be used preparatory to the feast of any saint, and therefore blanks are left. It is partly compiled from one in use in France.

any importance except in so far as you may avail yourself of it for the attainment of your last end. You ought to be perfectly indifferent to all besides. You ought to use, or to abstain from all creatures, simply with regard to your end. St. Colette understood this. Therefore having God always in view, she was completely indifferent to the honours or goods of the world; was wonderfully wise in her detachment from creatures, and practised perpetual self-sacrifice by the perfection of her poverty and obedience.

PRAYER.

O great saint, I admire the perfection with which you understood that God should be your all; that the world is nothing; and that we are only placed on earth, in order to love, revere, and serve Him. Obtain for me the grace to believe firmly that I have been sent into the world, not to amass riches, or to obtain the esteem of others, and still less to satisfy my bad passions, but to serve my God. Could I only understand this truth as you understand it, I should be truly wise. Beseech our divine Lord to grant me this grace, O

SECOND DAY.

On the motives which should induce us to meditate on our last end.

Consider how numerous, and how powerful are the motives which should induce you to meditate on your last end. On death, because you will certainly die. On judgment, because all your thoughts, words, actions, omissions, desires, motives will be judged by an infinitely holy Judge, from whom nothing can be hidden; who has seen and weighed all your actions. On hell, because there is a hell, and it must be my eternal abode if I die in mortal sin. On heaven, because there is a heaven, and it may be my home for eternity if I wish it. Death, judgment, hell, heaven, oh! my God what solemn words are these, and yet how seldom I reflect on them. Think on your last end, says the Holy Ghost, and you will never sin.

PRAYER.

Grant me, O my God, I beseech Thee, through the intercession of Thy saints, particularly [... .....] the grace to reflect seriously and constantly on these solemn truths, and to prepare myself in time for eternity.

THIRD DAY.

On considering our Last End.

Consider how important it is for us to be *firmly* determined to secure our eternal salvation, and to use all the means necessary for the attainment of this end. Why has God created the world, and all that is in it? Is it not to help you to attain your salvation?—Why did the Second Person of the blessed Trinity become man? Was it not principally for your salvation?—Why did Jesus Christ live a life of labour, suffering, and poverty? Was it not to assist you to enter heaven ?—Why does our divine Lord give you such tender tokens of His love in the Holy Eucharist, becoming there your Priest, your Victim, and your Food? Is it not still for your eternal welfare? Creation, Incarnation, Redemption, and Eucharist, how these four words should recall the love of my God, and urge me to occupy myself with my great, my only concern. In truth there is nothing of such importance for me;

nothing more pressing. Time is flying, death is approaching stealthily like a thief; tomorrow perhaps time will have ended for me. All will be lost, or all will be gained. How miserable am I if I am not in earnest in this all important matter.

PRAYER.

O great saint, who so ceaselessly and earnestly pursued the all important affair of salvation, obtain for me the grace to follow in your blessed steps. Under your powerful protection I desire this day to begin to live for eternity, and to use the things of time and sense only so far as they may assist me in securing my eternal welfare.

FOURTH DAY.

On the Evil of Sin.

Consider, sin is the only real evil. Let us contemplate some of the terrible effects of a single mortal sin. As regards God, it is the greatest outrage which can be offered to the Divine Majesty. It revolts against all the essential attributes of God. It insults His power, it rebels against His sanctity. It has, we may say, in a measure obliged the Eternal Father to deliver up His only Son to expiate its guilt; the Son to die upon the cross; and the Holy Spirit continually to strive against our corruptions. Then what evils has it not effected in the world; for one mortal sin millions of angels are precipitated from heaven to the lowest hell; and our first parents are expelled from paradise ; while to the end of the world, all men are subjected to sickness, suffering, labour, and death. Sin has opened hell, has separated souls eternally from God. And what has sin done for me? It has deprived me of grace, it has deprived me of merit, it has taken away the peace of my soul, it has blinded my mind, it has hardened my heart—well for me if it does not cost me a death-bed of anguish, and an eternity of misery.

PRAYER.

O my blessed Jesus, I cast myself at Thy sacred feet, and implore Thy mercy and compassion. I offer Thee the merits and prayers of Thy saints, and particularly of those who like the blessed Colette were singularly devoted to penance and reparation to Thy Divine Majesty, for the offences by

which Thou art so continually outraged.
Have mercy upon me, O my God, have
mercy upon me, pardon my sins, and with
the assistance of Thy divine grace, and
under the protection of my blessed patrons,
I will never more offend Thee.

FIFTH DAY.

Jesus Christ is the way to attain our End.

Consider how necessary it is for you to
be determined to imitate Jesus Christ.
Has He not a right to impose this obliga-
tion on you? He is your God, and all that
you have has been given to you by Him.
He is your Father, and what a Father! He
is your Saviour, and what a Saviour! He
is your King, and what a King! He has
purchased your soul for Himself in His own
blood. You are bound to Him by the most
solemn engagements. Would you be unfaithful to them? It is essential for your
happiness that you should love Him; vainly
will you seek for happiness in earthly
things. Happiness is only to be found in
God, because God alone is our End. Your
salvation requires it by a sweet, but in-
evitable necessity. No one can go to the

Father but through the Son. He is the way; out of Him we cannot attain our end. He is the truth; out of Him all is false and deceitful. He is the life; out of Him there is nothing but death.

PRAYER.

O my sweet Jesus, draw me, and I will run after Thee. Bind me to Thyself lest I wander from Thee. Oh! blessed Colette, fervent and ardent follower of Jesus crucified, obtain for me the grace fervently and ardently to follow Him in time, that I may be united to Him inseparably for all eternity. Amen.

SIXTH DAY.

Jesus Christ will lead us to our End.

We must not merely be convinced that it is necessary to imitate Jesus Christ, we must also study this divine model. Let us consider the principal virtues which He wishes us to imitate. First, His *interior* virtues. His love of humility; behold Him annihilating Himself in His Incarnation, and taking the form of a slave. His love of holy poverty; behold the King of glory born in a stable at Bethlehem. His love of dependence; in His flight into Egypt, and in offering Himself in the temple as a victim, ready to accomplish perfectly the will of His Eternal Father. Consider the virtues of His hidden life; His obedience to Mary and Joseph; His holy labours, for we are told that He worked as a carpenter with Joseph; His self-forgetfulness; He remains for thirty years hidden from the eyes of men. Consider the virtues of His public life. His love of God; He thinks only of accomplishing the will of His Father, He labours only to promote His glory. His love of souls; this is His first object after the glory of God. The cross is at once the means of glorifying God, and of saving the world; He embraces it, He dies on Calvary. Behold our Model. How am I endeavouring to imitate it?

PRAYER.

O blessed saint, whose life was so like to that of our crucified Saviour, obtain for me the grace to conform my life to this blessed model, and in all my actions to consider how my Jesus would have me to perform them. O good Jesus, I desire to imitate Thy blessed example; pity my weakness, and strengthen me in the good resolution with which thou hast so mercifully inspired me.

SEVENTH DAY.

On the Works which we must do in order to attain our End.

Consider that it is necessary for us to be earnest in good works if we hope to obtain an eternal recompense. We shall not be rewarded for the good thoughts we have had, nor for the good resolutions we have made, but only for the good which we have *done*. Not those who say, Lord, Lord, shall enter into the heavenly kingdom, but those who *do* the will of God. The kingdom of heaven must be taken by violence. Resolve, then, firmly to execute faithfully the following practices.

1. To exercise yourself constantly in acts of humility and mortification.

2. To be most exact and faithful in fulfilling all the duties of your state of life.

3. In regard to your neighbour to perform such acts of charity, spiritual or

PRAYER.

Oh my God, when I consider the fervour and devotion with which Thy saints have loved and served Thee, I am ashamed of my own coldness and tepidity. Have mercy upon me, O my God. O blessed saint, who ran in the ways of God with such unwearied zeal, obtain for me the grace to imitate your blessed example, that I may one day obtain a share in that blessedness which you now enjoy.

EIGHTH DAY.

On the means which will assist us in attaining our End.

The first means we should employ is prayer. Prayer is an essential duty. We must pray, for our divine Lord has recommended us to do so. If we do not pray we exclude ourselves wilfully from the kingdom of heaven. If we pray with faith, with confidence, with perseverance, we are sure to obtain what we ask, for our Lord has said, that whatever we ask the Father in His name He will give it.

The second means is still more efficacious,

because it confers of itself the grace we need; it is the frequentation of the sacraments of Penance and the Eucharist. The one remits our sins, and gives us an increase of sanctifying grace; the other in nourishing our souls with the body, blood, soul, and divinity of our Lord Jesus Christ, imparts to us the very source of grace.

The third means is the help and intercession of the saints, but above all of the ever Blessed Mother of God. We do not work alone in labouring for our salvation; we have near the throne of God a Mother who is infinitely good, and who loves us most tenderly; a Mother who is all powerful with God, and who is ever ready to lavish on us the greatest favours.

PRAYER.

The Hail Holy Queen, and three Hail Mary's, in honour of the special devotion of the saints of the Franciscan Order to our blessed Mother.

NINTH DAY.

On the Love of God.

Love is the fulfilling of the law. Consider then the immense love of God for His creatures, for you—in order to confirm yourself more and more in the good resolution you have formed. He has created the world for you, with all that is bright and beautiful in it. All things speak to you of His love. The sun by day, the moon by night, all are gifts of His love. His providence watches over all your steps. His love pardons your many wanderings. He has given His Son to save you; His Holy Spirit to sanctify you. And all He asks from you in return for countless and undeserved mercies is your heart. Surely you will no longer refuse to give it to Him. Approach then to-day if possible the sacrament of Penance, and tomorrow the adorable sacrament of the Altar. Obtain the forgiveness of your sins, and promise your divine Lord under the protection of the Immaculate Mother of God, and of this great saint, that you will henceforth love Him with your whole heart, and never more offend against His surpassing charity.

PRAYER.

Oh blessed saint [......] intercede for me that my confession may be sincere and penitent, my purposes of amendment effectual, and my communion fervent and devout. Sweet Jesus I come to Thee once more; Oh for the love of Thine own Immaculate Mother, grant me the graces which I ask and need. Pray for me, O blessed [......] that I may never again offend my good and loving God.

THE LITTLE OFFICE OF ST. FRANCIS OF ASSISI.*

AT MATINS.

℣. O Lord open Thou my lips,

℟. And my mouth shall declare Thy praise.

℣. Incline unto my aid, O God.

℟. O Lord make haste to help me.

Glory be to the Father, &c.   Alleluia.

Inv. Jesus Christ who has suffered death for us; O come, let us adore; and let us praise the devout compassion of Francis.

Ps. Venite.

O come, let us be glad in the Lord, let us joyfully sing to the God of our salvation: let us come before His presence with thanksgiving, and make a joyful noise to Him with psalms.

Jesus Christ, &c.

For the Lord is a mighty God, yea a

---

* This Little Office is translated from the original (attributed to St. Bonaventure) for the first time. It has been abridged in some places.

mighty King, above all gods: for the Lord will not reject His people; for in His hands are all the ends of the earth, and He beholdeth the heights of the mountains.

O come, let us adore.
Glory be to the Father, &c.
O come, let us adore.
Jesus Christ has suffered, &c.

HYMN.

O Infant Jesus, sweetest child,
    In a poor stable born,
Thou fillest the world with light and love
    Upon Thy natal morn.

Dear little Babe of Bethlehem,
    Thus Francis cries to Thee;
Breathing the name of Mary's Son,
    In sweetest melody.

O lily flower, amid earth's thorns,
    In fleshly prison bound,
The spotless Mother's spotless Son,
    In thee all joy is found.

To Thee be glory, sweetest Lord,
    By virgin Mother given;
To raise the fallen up from earth
    To Thy bright home in heaven.

Ant. As the morning star, so has Francis shone upon us, conquering the world, the flesh, and the devil.

Psalm 88.

The mercies of the Lord I will sing for ever.

I will show forth Thy truth with my mouth to generation and generation.

For Thou hast said: Mercy shall be built up for ever in the heavens: Thy truth shall be prepared in them.

I have made a covenant with my elect: I have sworn to David my servant: Thy seed will I settle for ever.

℣. This child shall be great before the Lord.

℟. For His hand is with him.

Absolution.—May the merits and prayers of the blessed Francis, and all the saints, bring us, O Lord, to the celestial kingdom.

Lesson.—Blessed Francis, most dear father, faithful guide of our host, intercede for us with the Son of Mary, that by thee He may give us refreshment, who has given thee to us.

℣. Thou then, O Lord, have mercy upon us.

℟. Thanks be to God.

AT LAUDS.

Ant. While thou wast weeping for the sorrows of Jesus thy beloved, the seraph marked thy body with light.

Psalm 64.

O God, my God, to Thee do I watch at break of day.

My soul hath thirsted after Thee: and my flesh, O how exceedingly!

In a desert land, and pathless, and where no water is; even as in the sanctuary I appeared before Thee: that I might behold Thy power and Thy glory.

For Thy mercy is better than life: my lips shall praise Thee.

Little chapter.—Like the terebinth I have spread out my branches: and like the vine, fruitful and sweet flowers.

HYMN.

The morning light now fills the sky,
Demons before it swiftly fly;
So the false joys of earth are driven
Before the eternal joys of heaven.
And now a seraph swift descends,
And on the saint his glance he bends;

Wounding him in his inmost heart
With outward, and with inward dart,
For which by all men now be given,
Praise to the glorious King of heaven.

℣. I am signed with the sign of the living God.

℞. In the house of them who loved me.

PRAYER.

Almighty and Eternal God, who by the glorious nativity of Thy only begotten Son, hast brought a remedy to a sinful world; and by the blessed Francis Thy confessor, hast recalled to the way of life many who wandered from it; grant us, that we returning from the way of error, may be restored by Thy grace.

AT PRIME.

In honour of the Call and Conversion of St. Francis for the welfare of the human race.

℣. Incline, &c.   Glory, &c.

HYMN.

The sun is lighting up the heavens,
   Let us with angels sing;
And chant the praises of our Lord,
   Our glorious blessed King.

Now to the world the light of Christ
    Does blessed Francis show,
While on his feet, his hands, his side
    Christ's blood red wounds do glow.

Ant. Behold a glorious new light is enkindled in the heavens.

Psalm 33.

I will bless the Lord at all times, His praise shall be always in my mouth.

In the Lord shall my soul be praised; let the meek hear and rejoice.

O magnify the Lord with me: and let us extol His name together.

I sought the Lord, and He heard me; and He delivered me from all my troubles.

Come ye to Him and be enlightened; and your faces shall not be confounded.

This poor man cried; and the Lord heard him, and saved him out of all his troubles.

Little chapter.—Blessed is he who reads and hears the words of this prophecy, and observes what is written therein, for the time is at hand.

℣. Light hath arisen for the just,

℞. And gladness for the true of heart.

PRAYER.

blessed Francis hast restored that which was
fallen, and hast instituted the rule of the
Seraphic Order, grant that following his
example we may serve Thee with free and
joyous hearts.   Through, &c.

AT TIERCE.

*In honour of the Institution of the Order
and Rule of the Blessed Francis.*

℣. Incline, &c.   Glory, &c.

HYMN.

O citizen of that blest land,
    Where God alone doth reign;
Teach us with Jesu's blessed name,
    To charm away each pain.

The odour of thy virtue now
    Like fragrance shed around,
That we, like thee, before our Lord
    May be as fragrant found.

That bearing with courageous hearts,
    Our cross with Christ our King,
Victorious songs in endless bliss,
    We too with thee may sing.

Ant. He founded three orders: the first
called Friars Minors; the second, the

Poor Ladies; and the third was for both sexes.

Psalm 18.

The heavens show forth the glory of God, and the firmament declareth the work of His hands.

Day to day uttereth speech, and night to night showeth knowledge.

The law of the Lord is unspotted, converting souls: the testimony of the Lord is faithful, giving wisdom to little ones.

Little chapter.—And whosoever shall follow this rule, peace be upon him, and mercy and upon the Israel of God.

℣. The just shall flourish as the palm tree,

℞. And shall spread abroad like a cedar of Lebanon.

PRAYER.

O God, who didst deliver Thy people from the hand of Pharao, and the bondage of Egypt by Moses; grant to us, that following our leader and being enrolled in his army, we may be led by him to the attainment of celestial joys. Through, &c.

AT SEXT.

*In honour of the constant prayer of St.
Francis, and his prophetic spirit.*

℣. Incline, &c.   Glory, &c.

HYMN.

O great, O glorious Trinity,
  Before Thy throne we bend,
And with this blessed saint to Thee
  Our adorations send.

Spurning the world's false joys with him,
  We weep the bitter grief,
Which Christ, our Love, upon the cross
  Suffered for our relief.

With ceaseless tears, both day and night,
  This bitter passion we
Will mourn within our inmost heart,
  Will mourn most tenderly.

Ant. He was inflamed with seraphic
love, and filled with the spirit of prophecy.

Psalm 41.

As the hart panteth after the fountains
of waters; so my soul panteth after Thee,
O God.

My soul hath thirsted after the strong living God, when shall I come, and appear before the face of God?

Why art thou so cast down, O my soul? and why dost thou disquiet me? Hope thou in God, for I will still give praise to Him: the salvation of my countenance and my God.

Little chapter.—He praised the Lord with his whole heart, and rejoiced in Him who created him, and his prayer was heard.

℣. Be thou faithful unto death,

℟. And I will give thee a crown of life.

PRAYER.

O Lord Jesus Christ hear us we beseech Thee, through the merits of our holy and blessed father, in whose flesh Thou didst wonderfully renew the sacred marks of Thy Passion, that we may continually experience its blessed fruit. Through, &c.

AT NONE.

In honour of the obedience of creatures to the Blessed Francis.

℣. Incline, &c. Glory, &c.

HYMN.

Seven times a day we'll chant his praise,
  Who all for Christ has given,
And now enthroned in glorious light
  Reigns with his Lord in heaven.

The birds and beasts his voice obeyed,
  And answered to his call;
His pure and lowly heart obtained
  A victory over all.

O Thou eternal Lord by whom
  All things exist and live,
To us with Francis ever more
  Eternal gladness give.

Ant. He shall rejoice in all things; he shall reign in glory.

Psalm 8.

What is man that thou art mindful of him? or the son of man that thou visitest Him ?

Thou hast made him a little less than the Angels, Thou hast crowned him with glory and honour: aud hast set him over the works of Thy hands.

Thou hast subjected all things under his

feet, all sheep and oxen: moreover the beasts also of the field.

The birds of the air and the fishes of the sea; that pass through the paths of the sea.

O Lord our Lord, how admirable is Thy name in all the earth!

Little chapter.—The Lord will make all flesh fear him; he shall rule over the beasts of the earth and the birds of the air.

℣. The Lord hath crowned him with glory and honour,

℞. And hath placed him over the works of His hands.

PRAYER.

O God who hast enlighted Thy Church by the merits and teaching of blessed Francis, grant that through his intercession we may receive eternal rewards. Through, &c.

––––––

AT VESPERS.

In honour of the impression of the Sacred Stigmata.

℣. Incline, &c. Glory, &c.

Ant. A mysterious cross shone over Francis, behind which two swords were crossed.

Psalm 116.

O praise the Lord, all ye nations: praise Him, all ye people.

For His mercy is confirmed upon us: and the truth of the Lord remaineth for ever.

Little chapter.—Behold, I, John, saw another angel ascending from the east, having the sign of the living God.

HYMN.

Glowing with the wounds of Christ,
　　Burning with seraphic fire;
See the blessed Francis stand
　　High amid the heavenly choir.

On his side, his hands, his feet,
　　See his Master's wounds impressed;
Who so glorious as our saint
　　In the land where all are blest?

Sing his praise, ye poor ones now,
　　Follow in his holy train,
So may you celestial joys
　　With your blessed father gain.

To the great and glorious Three,
　　Be unending laud and praise;
And to Mary, virgin blest,
　　Songs of sweetest joy we'll raise.

℣. Thou hast signed Thy servant Francis,

℟. With the sign of our redemption.

Prayer as at Prime.

AT COMPLINE.

In honour of the happy passage of Francis to eternity.

Convert us, &c. Incline, &c. Glory, &c.

Ant. O blessed father remember us before the throne of God, where thou art crowned eternally.

Psalm 141.

I cried to the Lord with my voice: with my voice I made supplication to the Lord.

In His sight I pour out my prayer; and before Him I declare my trouble.

Deliver me from my persecutors; for they are stronger than I.

Bring my soul out of prison, that I may praise Thy name: the just wait for me, until Thou reward me.

HYMN.

Celestial voices sweetly sing
The praises of their God and King,
The glory that the saints have given,
Who shine like stars in yonder heaven.

Victorious soldier, trophies bright,
They raise within the land of light,
Where every hour brings some new joy,
Where pleasure never can alloy.

Then let us join their happy lays,
And sing to God with voice of praise,
The victories and the combats won
By Francis, through His blessed Son.

Little chapter.—Be thou faithful unto death, and I will give thee a crown of life.

℣. Glorious art thou in the sight of the Lord,

℞. For He hath girded thee with beauty.

PRAYER.

O God, who hast made the blessed Francis an associate with celestial spirits, grant that by his merits and intercession we may attain the like blessedness. Through, &c.

A PRAYER USED DAILY BY THE POOR CLARE COLETTINES,

Said to have been given to St. Colette by an angel, who appeared visibly in the choir before the religious. This prayer is translated from the original copy still preserved at Besançon.

Hail Mary. Glory, &c.

Blessed be the hour in which the incarnate God was born; blessed be the Holy Spirit by whose operation Jesus Christ was conceived; blessed be the glorious Virgin Mary of whom the Word Incarnate was born; through the intercession of the glorious Virgin Mother, and in remembrance of the most sacred hour in which the Incarnate Word was born, may the Lord hear my prayers and accomplish my desires. O Jesus who art mercy and goodness itself, do not abandon me on account of my sins or punish me as I deserve, but graciously hear my humble prayer, and grant me the favour that I ask for Thy honour and the glory of Thy holy name. Amen.

PRAYER TO BE SAID BY THOSE WHO WEAR THE CORD OF ST. FRANCIS.

O Lord, my God, break all the bonds of

my sins, and unloose the chains of my iniquities, and grant that, wearing this cord of penance in honour of my blessed father St. Francis, I may obtain the remission of all my sins, and a share in his holy prayers and merits, through the infinite merit of the wounds and Passion of my Saviour Jesus Christ. Amen.

ANOTHER PRAYER.

O Lord, gird my heart with the cord of piety and continence, that blessed St. Francis interceding for me, I may always remain in the obedience of Thy commandments.

PRAYER OF ST. FRANCIS TO THE BLESSED VIRGIN.

Holy Virgin Mary, there is none like unto thee born amongst women, daughter and hand-maid of the Eternal King of our heavenly country; holy Mother of our Lord Jesus Christ; spouse of the Holy Ghost; pray for us with St. Michael the archangel, with all the celestial powers, and with all the Saints, to thy most holy Son, our most dear Lord and Master. Glory be to the Father, and to the Son, and to the Holy Ghost. As it was in the beginning is now, and ever shall be. Amen.

HYMN FOR THE FEAST OF THE STIGMATA OF ST. FRANCIS, SEPT. 17TH.

On Alverno's lonely mountain
  See the blessed Francis kneels;
Pouring forth his heart's deep sighing
  Till the wounds of Christ he feels.

All he asks is still to suffer,
  And to love his Lord yet more;
And that all may know and love Him,
  As the sins of all He bore.

Evening comes and finds him praying,
  Praying on that lonely hill;
Morning dawns, and yet that blessed
  Blessed saint is praying still.

But his prayer is heard and answered
  Far beyond all human thought;
From the highest heaven a seraph
  Has a glorious message brought.

Now the blood red wounds are glowing
  On his hands, his feet, and side;
Now he stands the living image
  Of his Jesus crucified.

Oh! thrice happy, oh! thrice blessed;
  Dearest father pray for me,
That at least in heart, and spirit,
  I. Christ's wounds, may bear like thee.

HYMN FOR THE FEAST OF ST. FRANCIS.

High amid the choirs of light
  Where the highest seraphs soar,
There the blessed Francis stands
  Loving Jesus evermore.

Now no more shall earthly grief
  Dim his eyes with painful tears;
Now no more his spirit sink
  'Neath the weight of earthly fears.

Saintly father, we before thee,
  Wait, with weeping, for thy prayers ;
Saintly father, oh remember
  Those who struggle 'mid earth's cares.

Thou hast fought, and thou hast con-
      quered ;
  But for us the strife remains ;
Speed then gentle saint to help us,
  Lest we sink beneath our pains.

By thy thirst so deep, so burning,
  For the wounds of Christ thy Love,
On our needs one kind glance turning,
  Help us till we come above.

By thy heart, so kind and gentle,
  By thy tender, thoughtful ways,
By thy most unearthly raptures,
  By thy ecstasies of praise.

By thy weary, ceaseless vigils,
  By thy constant care and strife,
Whilst thy body here subduing
  Bring us to the land of Life.

By our blessed Mother Mary,
  By her heart, so dear to thine,
Holy father hear our pleading,
  To thy children's prayer incline.

We are pining, we are striving,
  But for thee the strife is o'er;
Help us, then, most blessed Father,
  Bring us to the golden shore.

There with thee for ever praising
  God the Father, Spirit, Son ;
We will sing, our joys unending,
  While the ceaseless ages run.

INDULGENCES

1. When they receive the Cord, they gain a plenary indulgence, granted by Sixtus V. and Paul V.

2. For confessing and receiving, and doing the prescribed works on all the feasts of our Lord, of our blessed Lady, of all the twelve Apostles, of St. John the Baptist, of All Saints, and of the principal saints of the order of St. Francis, they gain a plenary indulgence, granted by Innocent VIII., Gregory XIII., Sixtus V., Paul V. Innocent XII., and other Roman Pontiffs.

3. For accompanying the blessed sacrament to the sick, five years and five quarantines of indulgence. Sixtus V. and Paul V. in his bull, given the 11th of March, 1607.

4. For relieving charitably the poor, a hundred days' indulgence. Sixtus V. and Paul V.

5. For making peace between enemies, a ;

hundred days' indulgence. Sixtus V. and Paul V.

6. For saying the Office of the blessed Virgin Mary, or any other Office, or for being present when they are said, a hundred days' indulgence. Sixtus V. and Paul V.

7. When they assist at the monthly processions, and that they confess and receive that day, a plenary indulgence. Sixtus V., Paul V., and Innocent XI.

8. If they do not confess and receive, and yet will assist at the said procession, three years and so many quarantines of indulgence. Paul V.

9. For confessing and receiving on the principal feast of the confraternity, plenary indulgence. Paul V.

10. For hearing Mass in any of the churches or chapels of the Friars Minors, no any day of the year, forty years and three hundred days' indulgence. Alexander IV. and Clement IV.

11. For hearing Mass, or devoutly visiting the said churches any Saturday or Sunday of the year, eighty years' indulgence. Nicholas V. and Benedict X.

12. For hearing a sermon in any of th

said churches, six years' indulgence. Alexander IV. and Clement IV.

13. For one quarter of an hour's meditation, or mental oration, called the 'Way of the Cross,' a hundred days indulgence. Innocence XII.

14. For half an hour, or even a quarter of an hour's meditation every day for a whole month, and then confessing and receiving, plenary indulgence. Innocent XII.

15. For using the spiritual exercise for space of ten days, and at the end confessing and receiving, plenary indulgence. Paul V. But Alexander VII. granted the same indulgence perpetually to the Friars Minors, and so to those of the Cord, if they use the same exercise for the space of eight days.

16. For saying, or hearing the first Mass of a new made priest, if they confess and receive, plenary indulgence. Paul V.

17. For visiting the churches of the Friars Minors, and praying for the peace and concord of Christian princes, &c. all the indulgences of the stations of Rome. Paul V.

18. For going to preach, and convert infidels, or heretics, as well when they

prepare to go, as when they enter among them, plenary indulgence. Paul V.

19. For saying five Paters and Aves before any altar, on any day of the year, five years and as many quarantines of indulgence. Paul V.

20. When any one, or more of the Friars Minors shall celebrate Mass of the Dead for the soul of any brother of the Order of St. Francis, or for the souls of their parents, or for the souls of such who charitably lodge and receive the said Friars Minors, such soul shall obtain indulgence, so that it may be freed from the pains of purgatory. Clement VIII.

21. By saying five Paters and Aves, wherever the brethren or sisters happen to be, in honour of the five wounds of Christ, and the stigmas of Francis, when they cannot conveniently come to any of the Franciscan churches, they gain all the indulgences granted to the Friars Minors for visiting their own churches. Gregory XV.

22. For saying the Crown of our Lady of Seven Tens, plenary indulgence. Julius II., Leo X., Paul V., and Innocent XI.

23. For saying the Crown of our Saviour of Three Tens, plenary indul-

gence. Julius II., Adrian VI., and Innocent XII.

24. For saying the station of the blessed sacrament, plenary indulgence. Julius III., and Innocent XII.

25. For saluting one another with these words, "Praise be to Jesus Christ;" as likewise for answering, Amen, or For ever, or Always, fifty days' indulgence. Sixtus V.

26. For calling reverently the name of Jesus, or Mary, fifty-five days' indulgence. Sixtus V.

27. For saying devoutly the litanies of the blessed name of Jesus, three hundred days' indulgence. Sixtus V.

28. For saying devoutly the litanies of our blessed Lady, two hundred days' indulgence. Sixtus V.

29. For kissing devoutly the habit of the Friars Minors, five years and so many quarantines of indulgence. John XXII.

30. All these indulgences the brethren and sisters may apply and impart to the souls in purgatory. Sixtus V., Paul V., and Gregory XV.

31. At the hour of death invoking the name of Jesus, with the mouth or heart, plenary indulgence, Sixtus V., and Paul V.

32. For being buried in the habit of St. Francis, plenary indulgence. Clement IV., Nicholas IV., Urban V., and Leo X.

Funiculus Triplex.

CONTENTS.

1 DE63

Life of Anna Maria Taigi, A Holy Woman who attained, in the Married State and amidst the cares of a Family, and the train of poverty, to such Eminent Sanctity, that the process of Her Canonization is now going on at Rome; her Husband and some of her children giving evidence of her Heroic Virtues. She died in 1837. Translated from the French and Italian lives written by the Rt. Rev. ......, Bishop of Hasebon. By a Sister of Providence. ..... royal 32mo, printed wrapper, One Shilling—Cloth gilt edges, 1s. 6d.

Life of St. ...... of A....., with a Sketch of the ...... Order; by a Religious of the Order of Poor Cl... . Penned and Edited by Rev. W. H. Anderson, M.A. Permissu Superiorum, price 3s 6d

Hymns for Children, by a Religious of the Holy Order of Poor Clares, large royal 32mo., price 6d.

Funiculus Triplex: or, the Indulgences of the Cord of St. Francis. By the Rev. Father Francis Walsh, S.J. pr....l.

The Cord of St. Francis, price 6d.

The Holy Ladder of Perfection, by which we may Ascend to Heaven. By St. John Climacus Abbot of the Monastery of Mount Sinai. Translated by Father Robert, Mount St. Bernard's Abbey Leicestershire, frontispiece demy 18mo 3s 6d

Nine Considerations on Eternity, by Jerome Drexelius, S.J. from the Latin of the Bavarian edition of 1620, by Father Robert of Mount St. Bernard's Abbey Leicestershire. Permissu Superiorum. Large royal 32mo frontispiece superfine cloth lettered 2s 6d

Easy Method of Preparation for a General or Particular Confession, suited for Missions or Retreats royal 32mo 2d

New Catholic Tale of great interest.

The Massingers; or the Evils of Mixed Marriages. By M.A.D. Dedicated (by permission) to His Eminence Cardinal Wiseman, post 8vo price 3s 6d